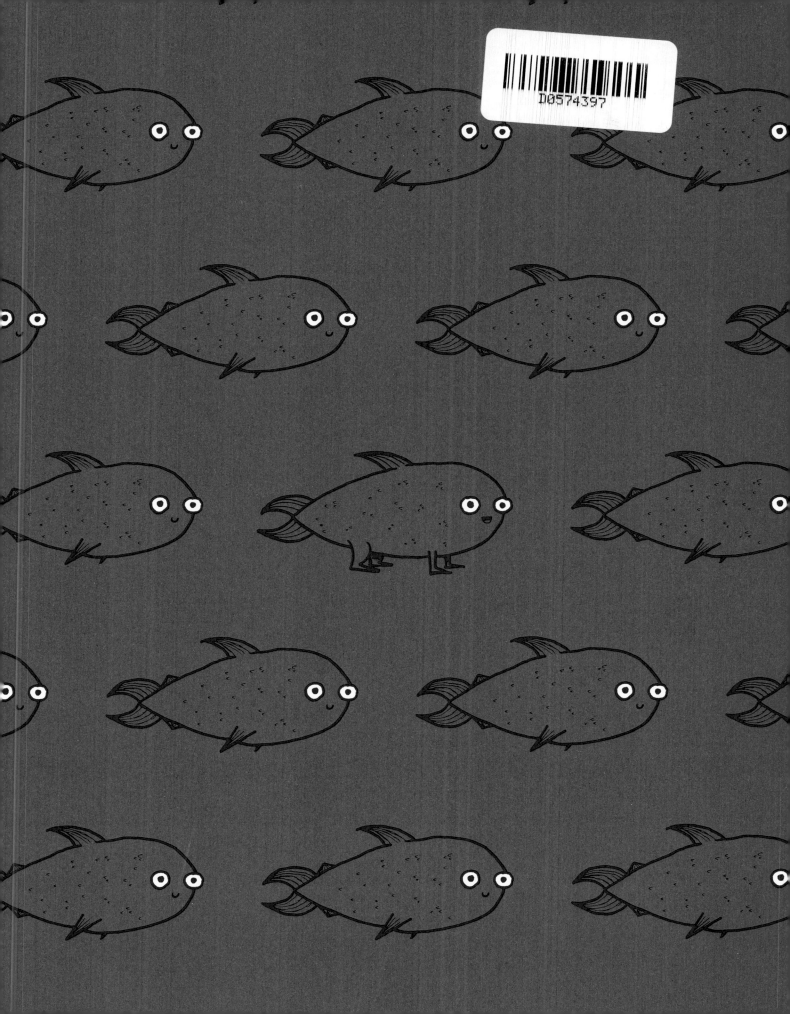

I USED TO BE A FISH

BY TOM SULLIVAN

Balzer + Bray

An Imprint of HarperCollins*Publishers*

I used to be a fish.

But I got tired
of swimming.

So I grew some legs.

Out of the water
and on land,
I changed even more!

I liked walking around and seeing new things.

But some of
those things liked
seeing me, too!

So I grew some fur,
and I learned
how to hide.

One day there
was a BOOM!

And things got a
little crazy.

After it calmed down,
I grew and changed
some more.

I liked swinging from trees and eating their fruit.

As time passed I got
taller and smarter, too.

But I lost
all my fur.

And bananas just
weren't cutting it
anymore.

So I went hunting
for some meat.

I drew all my
adventures
on the walls
of my cave.

The cave wasn't very cozy, though, so I built a hut.

And then a house.

You'd think I would
have stopped there,
but I kept building
and building.

Who knows
what's next?

Maybe I'll fly—
that's my wish.

Until then,
I'll have to
settle for this.

And the
funny thing is,
I used to be a fish.

A BRIEF HISTORY OF LIFE ON EARTH

The Earth is very, very old. By comparison, humans haven't been around for all that long. Imagine if the Earth were one hundred years old; modern humans would have been around for only 1.98 days. That's not even forty-eight hours!

 3.8 billion years ago: Simple Cells

 EARTH: 4.6 billion years ago

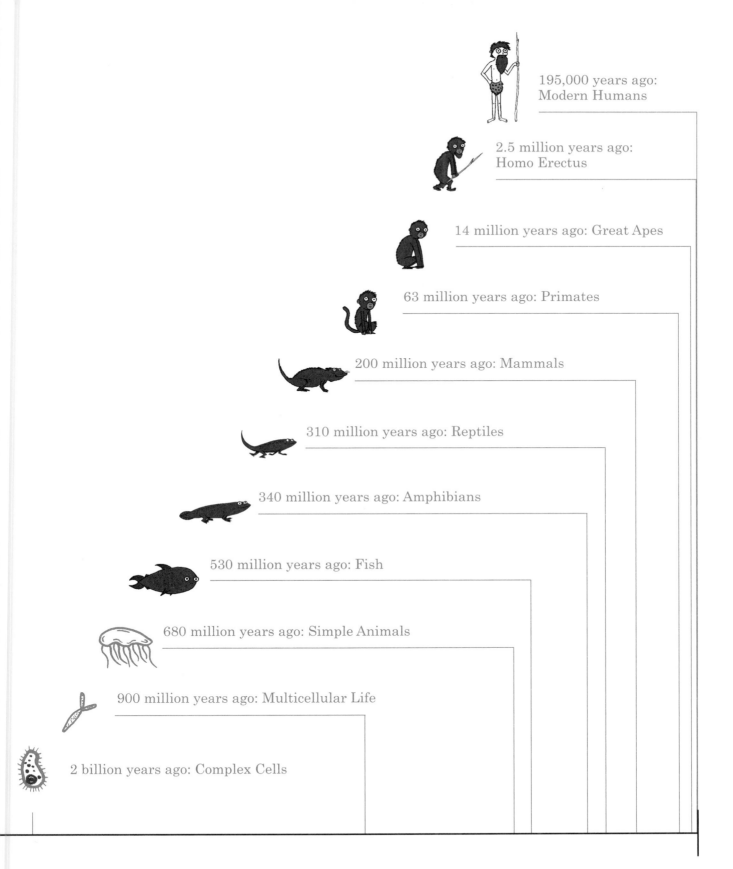

195,000 years ago:
Modern Humans

2.5 million years ago:
Homo Erectus

14 million years ago: Great Apes

63 million years ago: Primates

200 million years ago: Mammals

310 million years ago: Reptiles

340 million years ago: Amphibians

530 million years ago: Fish

680 million years ago: Simple Animals

900 million years ago: Multicellular Life

2 billion years ago: Complex Cells

EARTH: Today

AUTHOR'S NOTE

evo·lu·tion [ˌevə'loōSH(ə)n] *n.*
1. the process by which different kinds of living organisms are thought to have developed and diversified from earlier forms during the history of the earth; 2. the gradual development of something, especially from a simple to a more complex form

I Used to Be a Fish is a fictional story inspired by the science of evolution. Here are some facts you should know about evolution, according to the first definition of the word:

- The process of evolution doesn't happen to one single organism over the course of its lifespan; rather, it occurs over generations to entire populations of creatures—it's a very slow process.

- If you tried to illustrate the process of evolution, it would not look like a neat, straight line but more like a tree with many complicated branches. For example, some early fish evolved into amphibians, some amphibians evolved into reptiles, and some of those evolved into dinosaurs, which in turn evolved into today's birds. But some of those early reptiles evolved into the first mammals, and from those early mammals evolved horses, elephants, primates, and countless other animals.

- Evolution doesn't happen because a creature wants it to! (Though wouldn't that be nice if it were true?) In my book, a fish decides to grow legs—but in real life, such changes are unplanned.

- Just because something has evolved doesn't necessarily mean that it has gotten any better. The mutations that help drive evolution occur whether they benefit the organism or not.

The scope of my character's imagination, on the other hand, is absolutely true! Every one of us evolves (see definition number two) over our lifetime—we grow and change and dream big—and sometimes we even surprise ourselves by what we can achieve.

This book is dedicated to that brave little creature
who first set foot on land.

A very special thank-you to Glenn Branch of the National Center
for Science Education for his expertise.

And thanks to Steve, Donna, Hannah, Dana, and everyone else
who helped make this book possible. Especially Mom and Dad.

Balzer + Bray is an imprint of HarperCollins Publishers.

I Used to Be a Fish

Copyright © 2016 by Tom Sullivan

All rights reserved. Manufactured in China.

No part of this book may be used or reproduced in any manner whatsoever without
written permission except in the case of brief quotations embodied in critical articles
and reviews. For information address HarperCollins Children's Books, a division of
HarperCollins Publishers, 195 Broadway, New York, NY 10007.

www.harpercollinschildrens.com

ISBN 978-0-06-245198-9

The artist used Sharpies and Photoshop to create the illustrations for this book.

Typography by Tom Sullivan and Dana Fritts

16 17 18 19 20 SCP 10 9 8 7 6 5 4 3 2 1

❖

First Edition

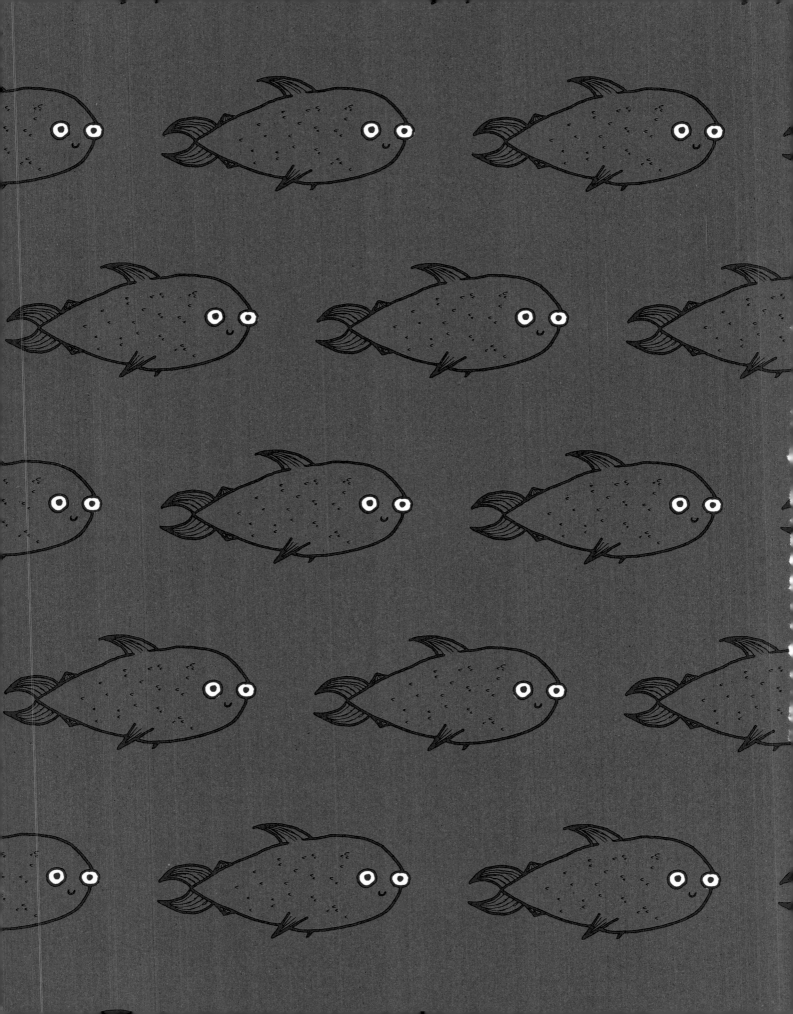